STORIES TOSSED IN OIL

Logan Marsh

MILTON & HUGO L.L.C.
4407 Park Ave., Suite 5
Union City, NJ 07087, USA

Website: *www. miltonandhugo.com*
Hotline: *1- 888-778-0033*
Email: *info@miltonandhugo.com*

Ordering Information:
Quantity sales. Special discounts are granted to corporations, associations, and other organizations. For more information on these discounts, please reach out to the publisher using the contact information provided above.

Library of Congress Control Number: 2024912337
ISBN-13:   979-8-89285-166-4   [Paperback Edition]
                  979-8-89285-165-7   [Digital Edition]

Rev. date: 05/28/2024

A man questions the seemingly perfect world around him, a pizza boy delivers to the same house for seventy years, a woman tries to remember the moment she fell in love, a sniper walks through a graveyard he helped to create, and a follower of his favorite color meets his undeserved end. Five tales spanning worlds and different types of people. Tragedy, complex emotions, obsessive love, relevance, and attempts to achieve some sort of relief in a dark world are why these stories have all been *tossed in oil*.

You may feel or have felt that you can never seem to do anything right, that no matter what you do, a dead end is always around the other corner. Suffering is guaranteed throughout life, no matter what genre you are in, no matter what story takes place, bad things will always happen, but it's how we adapt and change that leads to a happy ending for all of us.

*Minor swearing, violence, and heavy topics, PG-13

THE GARDEN

What happened here? Eddy kept asking himself this as he walked around what used to be the perfect home for any man like him. The garden was perfect in every sense of the word: It offered enough food to last eons, enough animals and pets to never be lonely, and the weather was always perfect and peaceful. But lately, there was more skin, flesh, and food than there was actual nature in the garden. Everywhere the man looked, people were gorging. Stuffing their faces with the fruit of the creator, doing sinful things to anyone they came across, and not a single person thought anything of it.

Chaos, utter chaos. Where was the sanctity? Where was the dignity? Most importantly, where was Aurther? Aurther was, presumably, the first person here. He lived as many do nowadays—doing as he pleased when he pleased and nothing ever came about. But Aurther was gone. No one knew where he went; nonetheless, he was gone. It was so hard to remember the names of people here that any one of the people around this garden could have been Aurther. People think it was when the creator made the first women that more people showed up. But it didn't matter—humanity was here now, and it was never going back to what it was before.

Eddy was most concerned about this compared to anyone here. He feared the creator more than most people. Aurther always maintained that eating and mating too much would make the creator mad and that we shouldn't use the gifts he gave us for granted, because ultimately he wanted us to be happy. Some gifts they were, indeed. Berries as big as your head, green pastures as far as the eye could see, lakes that were crystal clear—and none of it ever ran out. In each lake was a tall pink building of odd architecture and shape; they housed the most comfortable beds and furniture that could be sat on. No one ever fought or was sad. It was paradise.

Lately, however, many of the animals had been in the center of the garden, doing what Eddy did throughout most of the day, walking in a circle. The cows, the pigs, and the chickens had disappeared once man realized they could eat them. The other ones were undesirable. Dogs, leopards, and larger animals all circled the center of the garden, waiting. They walked and walked and walked, never slept, never ate, never enjoyed any of the pleasures of man. They simply walked. People would even ride the animals from time to time like in a merry-go-round. It was perplexing, to say the least. However, many didn't care at all and would just go back to indulging themselves after seeing something strange like that. Not Eddy. No, he was different. He was going to be happy, he was going to use these gifts as they were meant to be used, and when the creator came back, Eddy would finally be happy.

Eddy's questions would never be answered, nor would he ever talk to anybody else about these. He was simply trying to think about them and solve them on his own. Trying to think about the faults of man. Too bad it was so hard to think with that damn ringing in his ear. It had persisted all throughout this morning but it never went away. Every time he tried to think about the last time he saw Aurther, it would just get louder and louder until he had to stop walking. It was unbearable. It grew louder with, every step he took, and his sight was fading and it just made him want to scream.

"Hey, you gotta try this!"

"W-what?" The ringing went away, and he looked around for the person who asked him that, and he saw a short fat man with red hair. The man's breasts drooped. You could tell he didn't miss any meals. He was eating a large red berry that was plump and juicy. Eddy couldn't tell who was who.

"This stuff is so good. It makes you feel warm inside and gives you more energy to eat even more!"

Logan Marsh

"Uh-oh, no thanks, I'm full."

"Ha, more for me, then." He went back to eating.

A woman then walked up to them, and they started eating together. Eddy went back to walking in the garden. The exchange meant nothing because Eddy meant nothing. Truly, he was as significant as the berry the man was eating, just another morsel in an endless feast for man. Eddy was disgusted and distraught. Was he wrong about the way he lived? Of all the things he was sure of, he was sure that he wasn't happy. He genuinely hated the paradise he lived in. It was gross. A matter of opinion, I suppose, but ultimately meaningless to the rest of humanity. Could he be happier living this ignorant lifestyle and forgetting about Aurther and the creator? Following the lead of his peers , could he turn over a new leaf for himself?

No!! he thought. Everyone was goners in the creator's garden, which was a test of will rather than a paradise. He would prove he loved the creator more than anyone—he would be the next Aurther. Sense, logic, obedience—everyone else ate huge berries all day, but the creator gave Eddy lemons, and he would make the sweetest lemonade he could. He would walk and walk until the creator loved him again, because clearly, he didn't if he let it get this bad. He would walk and ponder until he came back ... even if this stupid ringing wouldn't stop! Eddy was sweating, his knees were weak, and the ringing was horrible. The only other thing he could hear were the sounds of the man behind him—the burps, the chewing , the sex, everything that just made the ringing worse. *Why, why?!* he thought. Why would the creator do this to him? Why would he make such an awful garden with these horrible people in it?

Eddy was crying on the soft soil now, but no one noticed him in all their pleasure. He was begging for the creator to come back, looking at the sky and shouting, "SAVE US FROM THIS AWFUL GARDEN!" Why didn't the creator love Eddy? He did everything right. He never ate too much, he was a virgin, never did anything wrong, but still, the creator hated him. The ringing was at its loudest. He couldn't hear or see anything, and he was about to pass out.

The animals stopped, everyone's smiles faded, and the ringing ceased. Eddy got up off the ground. The sky had turned from a light blue to a sinister black. Strands of bright, hot orange filled the sky, the lakes turned to tar, and all the food rotted away. Eddy smiled and started shouting.

"Finally, it's the creator! He at last, the god of this garden, the father of us all, is here to save us."

The shouting, smiling man who once hated the glorious world around him had met his maker—no, his savoir.

But the creator wasn't here to save Eddy or the rest of humanity. He was here for his garden.

(Inspired by Hieronymus Boch's Garden of Earthly Delights.)

PIZZA BOY

A large pepperoni pizza with a cheesy crust and a side of breadsticks. An order he knew by heart, almost as well as the house he would deliver it to. The toppings spread accordingly on the surface of the pizza, cooked at a nice 500 degrees Fahrenheit, and the finest breadsticks the county of Helena had to offer. To many, an insignificant order at a minimum-wage job worked just to make ends meet for a high schooler, but to him, it was so much more. It would be his whole life. Working at Big Town Pizza made him happy, or rather, the prospect of gaining happiness even more so.

Connor had worked at Big Town Pizza for six years now, ever since his junior year. He was twenty-one now, and he had no intentions of going to college or finding a better-paying job. Why would he? He had everything he could want right here in town. A perfect job, family, and all the free pizza he could want. Getting fired wasn't only undesirable for him, it was also impossible, considering he was the best employee and knew more about this business than Tony, his boss. He got there at ten and left at seven, making pizza, helping customers, and cleaning. It was what it was, and he was happy, almost.

It was Thursday night, his favorite day of the week, and he was about to deliver to the best customers in the world. Connor knew that the Jeffersons lived busy lives, Mr. Jefferson was a professor at a university, and Mrs. Jefferson was a nurse at the local hospital, meaning that more than often, they didn't have time for a home-cooked meal, so more business for Big Town Pizza. They ordered the same thing nearly three times a week, but on Thursdays, she was home. He knew the route to their house by heart. He could probably drive there with his eyes shut, to be honest, and he would always arrive on time at six thirty. He threw in extra toppings on Thursday and made sure he showered and looked presentable. It wasn't just about the image of Big Town he was worried about—it was also the image of his reliability.

He parked his car on the street, checked himself in the mirror one final time, walked up to the Jeffersons' door, and rang the doorbell. Week after week after week, he would deliver but today would be different. Finally, he would say something other than the usual company slogan. It was time for him to confess; everything had been leading up to this moment.

The door opened, and out came a beautiful woman. She had long red hair that reached down to her waist, dimples, and quite a slim physique. She was the same age as the pizza boy in front of her and wore bright-red lipstick and held a cigarette in hand. She looked so much more mature than her age, and she looked this way only because she usually got back from her sorority's Thursday meetings.

"Big Town Pizza. A large pepperoni pizza with a cheesy crust and a side of breadsticks?"

Connor tried to look and sound as pleasant and appealing as he could.

"Yeah, thanks." She took out fifteen dollars and handed them to Connor.

She took the box and was about the close the door …

This was it—only one life to live, only one thing he had to do.

"Hey, um, can I tell you something?" he said this as his heart raced and his hands shook.

She turned around. "Yeah, what's up?" she said with a smile.

Was this interaction amusing to her? He hoped it was more than just a joke to her.

"I just wanted to say …"

Please, God, think of something … Please, God, think of something …

"If you ever need anything, then … um, Big Town is always here for you." He said this with a smile on his face, although on the inside, he felt as though he would throw up.

"Oh … uh, yeah, thanks." She smiled awkwardly and closed the door rather abruptly.

He had choked, and all he had to show for it was a five-dollar tip.

He walked away from the house defeated, tears starting to build up. He thought about this moment for months, years even. He blew it. He wanted this girl. Anna Jefferson was what would finally make him happy, make him finally feel safe and secure. He lied to himself. Every morning he told himself he enjoyed this. He told himself, his family that he enjoyed it, but he hated it with every fiber of his being. Pizza was among his least favorite food, maybe just because it was all he ate these days, and the owner and boss of Big Town, Tony, was always hard on him for seemingly no reason at all. Connor suspected it was because he came from French descent and Tony was Italian, but that was just theory among the employees at Big Town—of which there weren't many.

Very few people worked at that local pizza place for more than two years or so. Connor was truly alone. His parents hated him for never moving out and working a high school job for the rest of his life. He had no friends, and he never really talked to anyone at work. Connor opened his car door, got in, and put in his favorite cassette. The cassette always rewound every time it was over, so to Connor, it felt never-ending, much like his life—an infinite song of passion heard by no one but his ears.

Stupid … STUPID! he thought as it played. There was always next week, he told himself, and if not, next month, and so on and so forth. Connor didn't know when this desire to be with Anna began. He always thought they were meant to be together, but alas, he could never seem to get up the courage to say how he felt. He felt so lonely and isolated every day. When he woke up when he went to bed—it was all so dull. Nothing exciting, absolutely nothing, ever happened in his life. Only these once-in-a-couple-years attempts at conversation, although nothing fruitful would come of them. This would be the first of many times he tried to get close to Anna.

Connor was lonely, no question about it. A couple of years later, he was forced to move out of his parents' house, got a decent-sized apartment, and still worked the same job. Things had gotten better, however, one Thursday night. It was May 24, Connor remembered. Anna looked at his name tag and said "Thanks, Connor," before closing the door. It was a huge step in the right direction. Before he knew it, there would be a ring around their fingers, and he would be happy.

Connor was about to deliver his Wednesday-night pizzas when Tony called him into his office. It was more of a closet than an office, and when Connor walked into the dimly lit room, he noticed pizza boxes stacked as tall as him. Tony looked tired, as he usually was, but not visibly angry or anything like that. He had his usual cigar in his mouth, and he smelled of gin.

"Hey, Tony, you wanted to see me?" Connor said this quite casually. He and Tony weren't the greatest friends in the world, but when you work with someone for so long, you're bound to have a decent-enough relationship.

"Hey, Connor, yeah, I just wanted to talk to you. Are you all right?"

Connor reflected on himself. How was he? Well, he was away from his parents, and his relationship status with Anna was going great right now. He was pretty happy.

"I'm good, how are you?"

"I'm fine." Tony puffed on his cigar. "Connor, you know tomorrow will be your tenth year of working here, right?"

"Really?" Connor didn't know that. Eventually, he just stopped worrying about it and accepted that this was the job he had, wanted, and could do. He didn't really think he could do anything else.

"Yeah, it will be. I've only been in this business for seven years. You have me beat. Are you considering taking my job when I retire next fall?"

"No, not really, sir. I like what I do right now."

"That's what I thought, Connor. I like you. I like you a lot. I know I'm hard on ya sometimes—that's just the way I am. But I'm getting worried. I mean, ten years is a lot for a normal job, but this line of work isn't for most people, which is why I ask, are you okay?"

It was such an odd question to him.

"Yeah, I'm fine."

"Okay. I just didn't want another Freddie situation. Do your rounds and then lock up." He tossed Connor the keys to the restaurant.

"Okay. Thanks, Tony," Connor said as he was starting to leave.

"No, thank you, Connor," Tony said as he tossed his cigar butt in the trash.

Connor thought about this interaction for the rest of the night and the following day. *Freddie! How could he possibly compare me to Freddie?!* he thought. Freddie was a worker who started working for Big Town around the same time that Connor did. They went to the same school together but never talked or had classes together. Freddie was such an odd person, probably the strangest Connor ever met. He was short and had messy hair and incredibly pale skin. He had a glass right eye that always seemed to go the other direction, giving off a certain level of crazy. Freddie was barely a worker at Big Town Pizza; his parents forced him to join every non-sport activity at the school, so he worked only on the weekends and Thursdays, assuming there were no academic team competitions going on. He was never allowed to work, register, or deliver, because Tony thought he would scare the kids, and he usually cooked in the back. He always seemed to burn the pizza, and Tony would go off on him relentlessly. One time it was so bad a customer actually said to Connor, "Is everything okay back there?"

Unbeknownst to Connor, Freddie always looked up to him. It could have been because he was one of the highest academically performing students at their high school or the fact that so many girls asked him out and he turned them down with nothing more than a "No, thanks."

Freddie was insane. He stared off into space a lot, slept, and always looked as though he was about to burst into tears on the spot. His mom kept such a tight rein on him (his dad left when Freddie was young), and she expected nothing less than perfection from him. He was so stressed he often failed tests just out of fear, scared to bungle a single question. The whole school called him Freaky Freddie. But one winter, during their senior year, Freddie disappeared, leaving only a paper of resignation and a note to Connor. Connor still had the note in his car. It read,

Dear Connor,

I don't know if you know this but I've always wanted to be friends with you. You always seem to be so calm and collected all the time, and I deeply want someone like that in my life. I've driven far out west and plan to live in Utah, away from my crazy family, away from this crazy job, and away from the stresses of life. I have a cabin there that my father left me. I advise you too as well, quit your job, come with me, and finally live.

The address to the cabin was left with the letter, but Connor threw that away years ago. Freddie was crazy. Connor was sure that Freddie would have killed him if Connor went to go find him. However, he felt bad and kept the letter. When he was making his Thursday-night delivery to the Jeffersons, he couldn't stop thinking about Freddie. The smell of hot pizza filled his car as he drove his usual rounds, pondering the topic at hand.

Was he just as crazy as Freddie? No, surely not. He wasn't crazy. His mind was as free as a bird; nothing held him back, and he was happy, surely he was. Connor would not become like Freddie. No, he would be different; his life was going to be good someday. Unlike Freddie, Connor had his life in order, and he was clear about his future.

Connor then hit a mailbox while he was lost in thought. It scared the soul out of him, and he snapped out of it. He got out and examined it. It wasn't bent or bruised, just slightly off-center from where it was originally. Then he looked at the house that owned it, and his stomach dropped to his foot. The Jeffersons had an expensive house, more elegant than most on the block; to damage something of theirs was an act of war, considering their wealthy position in this county.

Sweating, he quickly got the pizza. The car's clock read 6:42 p.m. He was late. He bolted to the door, feeling as though he would throw up and how horrible of a person he was. Thoughts racing in his head of how he would be killed once he opened the door and how he deserved every bit of it. The ringing of the doorbell felt like chimes of church bells as his coffin was lowered—not that anyone would care or be at his funeral, he thought.

The door opened, and he felt sick. "Uh … Big Town Pizza. A large pepperoni pizza with a cheesy crust and a side of bread—"

It was Anna, crying. She was wearing the usual getup that she wore on Thursdays, but she looked awful, like she had been sobbing for hours. Connor didn't know what to say. She had always been this perfectly happy person; he had never seen her so distraught, never mind that many of their interactions lasted only about thirty seconds. He felt so bad.

"Are you okay?"

"Oh, yeah, I'm just having a bad day. Fifteen dollars right?" She asked it so casually.

"Uh, yes, fifteen." Connor felt like crying himself because of the guilt. Guilt in knowing that he caused this woman to feel like this. Guilt in knowing that an off-center mailbox would ruin his life forever. Guilt that the only thing he had to live for was gone, all because he ran into the mailbox of the girl of his dreams. He wanted to die, but before that, he had to make things right.

"I'm so sorry, ma'am. I was daydreaming, and I didn't mean to make you so upset."

"What?"

"The mailbox, I hit your mailbox … Isn't that why you are upset?" Connor was puzzled.

Anna smiled, and then started laughing. "Oh, it's fine. I'm not upset at you, you're good."

The color came back to Connor's face. Maybe there was still hope for him in this life.

"Oh, okay. Well, I hope you feel better. Enjoy your pizza."

"Yeah, thanks"—she paused—"Connor."

The mission was a success. The pizza was delivered, and the two distraught people somehow felt better about the lives they lived.

Life went on, and the two of them never forgot about this exchange. The world changed around him, yet Connor remained in his existence, made livable only by the memory of this exchange. Looking at a name tag was one thing, but remembering the person's name was another. Connor's life even got better as well. A new boss was hired after Tony left, and Connor pretty much had to do his job for him, so Connor often got bonuses from the boss as a way of saying thanks. He was able to pay off his car, and even get gifts for his parents that Christmas. However, hope and happiness, much like money itself, don't last forever.

Changes were being made in the Jeffersons' house. For one, Mr. and Mrs. Jefferson had since moved out and retired, giving the house to their eldest daughter. Soon came another visitor at the Jefferson household.

Tom. Connor had first seen Tom at the beginning of the summer after Anna had graduated from college and become a full-fledged working adult in this world that Connor despised. Tom answered the door from that moment forward. No more Anna, only bad tips now. And he took forever to come to the door (meaning Connor had to ring the doorbell twice), and he didn't even say thank you.

Tom's car was always there, even when Anna wasn't there. Tom stayed home. Anna worked and worked to maintain that house, and Tom did nothing. He was a leech, taking but never giving. Connor never hated another human being more than he hated Tom. He was good looking, yes, but under that charm was a sinister soul that could not be redeemed in any way. At least not in the eyes of a pizza delivery boy.

Connor had to wait—wait like he had never waited before. What else could he do? Every waking moment was more heart-wrenching than the last. Never given the slightest hope or anything that she still remembered him. Truly, she was all Connor had. His parents died last fall, and he was an only child with no friends. When you have so little to look forward to, you start to care about only one thing and one thing only. But what to do if you are deprived of that one thing? Pain was his new life.

Tom and Anna got married. Two kids flooded their house with toys and laughter, and pizza was still their dish of choice. Every Thursday was more dreadful than the last. Was this what hell was? Delivering for an undetermined goal? *Why won't these people eat anything on Thursdays that's not pizza!* he thought as he slammed the car door in defeat with the package in tow. But he couldn't stop—for just a sliver of hope, he couldn't stop. Somehow, someday he would be happy, and it would only happen with her. He was sure of this. It had to be this way. Some people lived for their jobs. Connor had to be one of these people.

The same order, the same time, the same house, and the same mundane existence over and over again. He lost track of time, he lost track of his health, Big Town was renamed as Cheesy Pete's at one point, and he had to greet Tom with "It's always easy with Cheesy Pete's." He was going mad, one horrible slogan at a time.

On his forty-seventh birthday, he felt he was about to snap. It was the worst day of the week, Thursday. He pulled into the Jeffersons' at 6:25 p.m. He couldn't even remember the pizza-making process or the drive over. It just felt as though he was on autopilot, drifting through his day. He looked at himself in the mirror of his car. His face looked fat, he had bags under his eyes, and his face was unshaven. His hair was also thinning. What used to be jet black was now a weird grayish color. Not that it mattered; the pizza wasn't affected by this, and that was all the Jeffersons cared about. The man who carried that delightful Italian pie was nothing to them, no more important than the grease stains on the bottom of the box. He went up to the door, and he was about to press the doorbell when he heard something peculiar.

Screaming, coming from inside. Connor thought it was music at first, but upon a further listen, he could hear Anna's voice from within. She was crying.

"Why do you do this to me? I work all day, and then I come home and you yell at me"

Her voice quivered, which was in stark contrast to Tom's imposing, seemingly drunken wrath.

"You haven't done a damn thing for this family. I'm always the one taking them to school, cleaning the house, and you don't show me as much as a thanks!"

A crash could be heard. A bottle of some sort had been broken.

"Please, Tom, don't hurt me."

Connor, heart racing, had to do the one thing he knew how to do best.

Ding dong.

"Who the hell is that?" Tom said from inside

He opened the door, and just as Connor thought he smelled of alcohol, Tom looked arguably worse than Connor. He looked as though he hadn't slept in weeks and seemed to stagger to the door.

"It's always easy with Cheesy Pete's. A large pepperoni pizza with a cheesy crust and a side of breadsticks?" He said it with a smile, but he was deathly afraid of the man in front of him.

"Oh … yeah, yeah, how much do I owe you?" He seemed to slur his words as he talked.

Connor attempted to look in from behind the man's shoulder. He could faintly hear crying coming from within, but he did not see Anna. The imposing man handed him the money. No tip, of course, but Connor was just surprised he knew where his wallet was in this drunken state.

Then the door closed, and Connor put a hand to his ear. He listened well, but he didn't hear anything—no screaming, crying, nothing. The family had gone to eat, as a family should. A million thoughts were swirling in his head. He felt more alive than he had felt in all his life, and then he walked away with a smile on his face.

Connor contemplated calling the police, but he didn't need to, because in just a week's time, they had filed for divorce, and Tom's car was gone from their driveway, just like that. A blink to Connor. Sure, it had been years since they were married, but to Connor, it felt like five minutes. He felt alive again, finally. The prospect of being happy had come up again. Anna was free from the shackles of her abusive marriage, and the man who idolized her above anything else was free as well.

So he waited, and waited, as he usually did. Perhaps a little too long. He knew that she needed time to heal, but this prevented him from making any moves. Come to think of it, Connor always had trouble making moves. He never knew what to say, sure he didn't have that much time to express how he truly felt about her, but even then, they had come from completely different walks of life. She lived an extravagant life with a job and two kids, but Connor had nothing of the sort. He had no way to make himself appealing to her. Eventually, the war rolled around. As the world changed, Connor didn't, he was always just this same person he had been since he was sixteen. His uncle had been a doctor for years, and after paying a considerable amount of money to create a fake illness in his nose, Connor dodged the war draft. He couldn't sleep at night thinking that he could die and never get to hold Anna in his embrace. This war lasted years. Many died; even people Connor knew had to leave their boring minimum-wage jobs at Cheesy Pete's just to fight, and die for nothing. People still needed pizza, though, so Connor kept saying to himself, *Somebody has to do it.*

The town where this dinky little pizza place operated had become a ghost town. Many places did in the country, but poor areas like the one Connor lived in suffered the most. He was old—embarrassingly old, to be honest. The thought of a man taking heart medication yet still making fourteen bucks an hour was absurd to many, but not to him.

Anna hadn't had the best life either. Both of her children had gone off to war and died. Much like Connor, she had no major relatives. She lived alone yet still ordered from her local pizza place all the time. She wanted a slice of her childhood, to be reminded of better times, to be reminded of the happiness she once had. Every Thursday she would eat alone, her old and frail fingers dipping her breadsticks into tomato sauce the same way she did as a kid. Connor never realized this in his lifetime, but he had given Anna something that no one else could—comfort.

Connor also had no idea of his own mortality. Eating nothing but greasy pizza and diet soda takes a toll on your body, and this would be his last delivery. He pulled up to the house he pretty much grew up around his whole life. It was odd. He had seen this house in his dreams, yet he never knew what was inside. Glimpses, yes, but he had never seen what was inside the house. Where did his life go? It seemed to fade away as each pizza was delivered. A food that can be eaten by many due to its size, it unites so many people, yet it had separated him from reality. Each step he took in

Anna Jefferson's house gave him pain—not only mental but also physical due to his age. She was there, standing on the doorstep, waiting for her order to arrive. Time had been merciful with her looks. She still had that hospitable and loving smile on her face, even now. He arrived, after much chest pain and with sweat on his brow, with food in hand.

He caught his breath and said the phrase he couldn't get away from, no matter how hard he tried.

"It's always easy with Cheesy Pete's—"

But then he stopped and remembered that she had ordered the same thing her whole life: "Here is your pizza."

Anna smiled, and Connor did as well. "Thank you." She took the pizza, as was her destiny.

"How much?" she said as she was reaching into her purse with her brittle old hands.

Connor had the distinctive urge to give it to her for free, almost out of pity for the current emotional state she was in and the fact that she was their best customer. Suddenly, she dropped her purse and put her arms around Connor.

He didn't know what to say. It was like a dream he was in. Logical thought and action just weren't in his mind at the moment, and all he could do was hug her back. His job was done, the pizza was delivered, and he finally felt happy. They held each other as tears filled their eyes, until she finally said, "I'm just so glad that ... you are real."

His heart stopped for joy, some say. His life was over. Whether or not he had taken his heart medication that morning and that was a contributing factor, no one cared. Connor died in the arms of Anna Jefferson, the happiest he had ever been in his life, finally feeling that someone was there for him. The pizza was cold, the sauce was spilled, and the breadsticks were for the birds of tomorrow.

Abigail's Heaven

This room smells awful. Simply awful. I hate this place. It feels as though I've been here forever. Its drab wallpaper, ugly furniture, and flickering lights make me feel old. I am old, but nobody likes to feel like that. My own age is a mystery to me. I forgot a couple of weeks ago, and now the dates of my life seem to get further away. I have dementia, one of the later stages I believe, a bit ago they told me I had it once I started forgetting conversations and people. The doctors all said the same thing—that I would die not remembering a thing. A terrible thing, truly, but don't mistake me for a moron, I still remember some things.

I remember where my toothbrush is. I remember my adopted daughter's name, and I still remember him. That lady comes by now and then, startling the life out of me, she brings me my medicine and then skedaddles off like I never existed. I don't remember her, but she acts as if she knows me. This retirement homeroom is my whole world. The telly plays all day and all night for me. I try my hardest to remember better times, but I really can't. It seems better than before, but I don't know, I think I scared that lady once or twice and that's why she won't talk to me. It's like being in one of those … what's the word? Juicers. You know, ya put fruits in, and it chops 'em up. It's like I'm in one, and once I stop swirling and everything starts looking clear, the juicer seems to come back on, and I lose my train of thought.

A cruel joke, yes. Except for one. I think of him from time to time. Somewhere in, uh, Ambrosia, I believe, when I was a young woman. Yes, he was there in a ballroom with me, and we danced together while the great jazzmen played and sang their songs. It seems so foggy, like trying to look through a pop bottle. He is always clear, though. Everything except his face.

He took me by my hands and never wanted to let go as we danced. He told me that if he could stop time itself, he would. He never wanted to leave the ballroom or me. I loved the way he put his hands around my waist. Like a life preserver in the open sea, I could cling on to him. What a dancer he was. Each step he made on the floor was elegant and precise like an angel's. His name wa—"

BZZZZ!

"Good morning, senior citizens. This is the day of our shuffleboarding tournament here at Oldies but Goldies Retirement Home. Make sure to put on a big smile and wish Wallace good luck on the courts today."

I hate that voice. They put a phone in my ceiling about a year ago and said they would give us more pep in our step. All it does is wake us up when we're trying to sleep, and it disrupts my train of thought. Oh dear, what was I thinking about again? I have no idea … Suppose I'll just watch the telly and forget. Seems to be the only thing I'm good at around here. Some people in this joint have it worse. They're so far gone into illness that they don't know how to eat or go to the bathroom. I have no one to even talk to anymore. I don't go out much, and I don't know anyone here at this retirement house. At least they give us good food, although they don't seem to want to talk to me all that much. I just wish I had someone to have a real conversation with, I suppose. All instances of talking in my world, in my small room are gone, and most likely won't come back. Fuzzy talking as well. I'm often slurring my words, and it deters people from talking to me. Not that I truly have much to say.

I've done all I want to do in this life, I think. I can't remember whether I was happy before my mind went kaput. But I don't fear death. No one in this building does. All that could be said has been said. All that could be done has been done. Shuffleboard, bingo, the food—it's all a distraction from the fact that we could drop dead at any moment, but none of us seem to mind. At least I don't. My mind has already gone. I simply have to wait for the rest of me. Only one thing keeps me here. When I forget it, surely I shall die.

Some people write things down, some take pictures. I listen to music to help me remember. When I hear a song, I feel a sense of familiarity. My record player has one record, and I play it from time to time, scratched sounds and all. Then I'm back in the room. The room seemed to stop time as we spun around, dancing. The only thing keeping me from getting lost was him. His beautiful gaze, warm body, and strong exterior were heavenly. What a dancer he was: Each step was articulated with such precision, yet each was unique and beautiful in its own way. An angel he was. My sweet angel. But try as I might, that face is unclear. Great dresser he was, yes, but his face is unclear to me.

That name what … what was it now? He loved me, more than anything. His facial features are unknown, but his words feel familiar, like a song you've heard a thousand times before. Every time we would dip and come back up to the ballroom, he would kiss me. Oh well, the name doesn't matter, because he was there, and I was too, and we were happy. And once I forget being happy, I shall die.

It wasn't all bad. Being old was a gift in some ways. Simple things, really. Bird watching, seasons changing around you, and the telly to keep you company. I don't mind being old, I do mind being nearly brain-dead. I feel like an idiot, like I can't do anything without a reference point of some sort, or someone holding my hand. Freedom and independence were pipe dreams for people like me. Drifting—that's all I'm doing. What had I done to deserve this? I was good throughout my whole life. Where had he gone? … Oh, you know … the big one. God had left me, with nothing but a brain-dead existence and a ringing in my ear. Brittle bones that can't write, a room without a phone—I can't contact anyone. It's a small world. I was incoherent. No wonder no one wants to talk to me: I start talking about one thing and then move on to the next. I just seem to jump all over the place in conversation.

Marceline was supposed to come by, and she is late. Yes, I love her, but she doesn't love me. Waiting for me to die so she can take all my money and possessions, I'm sure. At that moment, the door is unlocked, and in comes that woman.

"Well, aren't you going to say something?" I shout as she opens the medicine bottle she has with her and starts putting them in my pill organizer. Ugly girl, ugly girl she is, snooping around stealing my stuff.

"When he gets back, he'll get you!" I shouted at that fiend of a lady.

"What do you mean, dear?" She has fear in her face, the sign of a criminal.

"All you do is come here, and you never say anything. Who the hell are you? I've no idea who you are, only that you come by and give me my medicine. Say something to me, please. I just want to feel alive!"

She pauses, and tears come to her eyes. "Come on now, let's turn on your record."

She sits me down and goes into the kitchen. She seems very upset. Not that I care. She puts the record on, and I am back. She makes tea in the kitchen as the trumpets play, accompanying the delightful rhythm and heavenly poetry of the great dead musicians of my time. He comes into view. It's clear—white dress against his black suit.

We danced and we danced. Our lives were never better before or after.

Sobs from the kitchen or the record, I don't care. he was here, I could almost make out his face.

Finally ... I can finally go. Be happy in the ballroom with him forever as the music plays. Scratches, fuzzy sounds, foggy noise—the record is my savior. I love him. I love him more than anything in the world. I would do anything to be with him again. I just want him to be happy. I don't know why he went away. I'm not sure if he ever did, but I still love him even now. I just wanted to hold him and never let go. If I let go, I would forget. If the dance goes sour, I will fall. If the music stops, I shall die.

I'm woken by a hug, but not from him. It's the lady. Even she can't ruin this moment for me. That thief can have her hug and then get out.

She wipes the tears from her face and leaves. Good riddance. All I need is him. Only he can make me happy. Oh, happy day, I shall pass on soon. No more forgetting, no more being another cog in this nursing home, no more being a bad mother to Marciline. She never comes by. Another day passes when she's not here. I'm surprised I haven't forgotten about her. Maybe tomorrow.

Why must it be this way? The end of my life as I know it, and I don't feel anything. I feel either sadness or remorse for my Marciline, who I'm leaving behind. A cruel joke, yes. It's funny, really. I still feel as though I am me, who has been here since the beginning. I still love her, and I still love him. The beautiful violin shall stop on the record, the needle will come up, and the ballroom shall spin no more. I'll go with him, and we'll be happy just me and him. Although I don't remember his name, his face, or his profession, I'll always remember his dancing.

Then the music stops, and I seem to have lost my train of thought.

JAZZ HANDS: A MOBSTER'S EPIC

Jazz Hands' grip on the Seattle crime scene can be traced back to when he first opened up the first Pretty Lady Land in a beat-up part of the city. The Miller mafia dealt in cigarettes and alcohol distribution; we dealt in things that people just couldn't get away from. But his goons dealt in, let's just say, a much more physical attraction. Cigarettes made Frank Miller a king in the fifties to the late seventies, but it was the eighties now, and Jazz Hands was on top. Tonight, he would fall.

My name is Vincent. I've been working with the Seattle Mafia for about seven months now and have become a prominent figure when it comes to sniping jobs. Any target, any distance, I could get him for you as long as you can pay. I'm part of the Miller family—I say family because that's what this mafia is, a family, consisting of Frank on top, buyers and lower mobsters next, and then us four at the bottom of the hierarchy. We have a huge job tonight, probably the biggest we've seen yet—so big that we've been camping out in a van for the past four hours playing blackjack to pass the time. At eleven o'clock on the dot, I would have to take myself up to the apartment building we are parked near, and the plan would unfold.

"You boys are almost ready," Fred said from his little slump on the ground. He was surrounded by radios and telephones, keeping a look out for police broadcasts and Frank checking in on the phone.

"Let's get this over with," I said, hopping out of the van.

"All right, see you in the next ten minutes, Vin," I heard Roger say from the front seat.

I love these guys a lot. I seem to have known them for only a short time, but I care about them a lot. Not so much Frank—maybe it's just because he yells so much—but I like the men in the van. The stairs of the building bring back memories of other operations we've done together. Roger is Frank's nephew, and he is the least experienced out of us all. I've worked in crime groups before and have been shooting rifles since for as long as I remember, but Roger hasn't had a lot of experience on the job. He loves his uncle, though, and he's a smooth talker, which would come in handy tonight. All he does all day is drink. It's a miracle he's sober today, and he's a pretty thin guy with good-looking hair, at least compared to his uncle. If anybody in Frank's gang of cronies were to be fired, it would be Roger first—mainly because he's a screwup to the rest of his family, including Frank.

Fred used to go to school with Frank, and both of them seem to be good chums. Fred's been to prison more than any of us, and he usually takes the fall for Frank a lot. Just shows you how good of a friend he is. He totally knows it all when it comes to radios and things like that, rigging the van and everything all by himself. We all have walkie-talkies so we can communicate back to him whenever. Fred's a nice guy, but you can tell he wants to be more than just the guy in the van. I think he acts nice to Frank because he wants a better position in the family, but that comes only when somebody above him is out, so Fred is gonna have to wait awhile for that to happen. He has thick glasses, kinda like a bug.

But the strangest-looking one out of all of us was Victor. He had a huge head of hair, all the way down to his shoulders, and you could barely see his eyes half the time, kinda like a walking mop in a tux. Whenever he talked, his breath would blow his hair out of his face. Don't mistake him for some hippie, though, because he was a coldhearted killer. I don't know how many guys he's whacked, but he's gotten them in nearly every way possible—guns, bats, knives, hell, I heard from Fred he beat the crap out of a guy with a mace one time. He's the best hitman in the whole East Coast, but he likes running with us nowadays. He could take out an entire mob in just a couple of minutes. He doesn't say much, but when he does, it's usually really polite and nice. Frank relies on him a lot—interrogations, whacking, and even dinners. He is always there to keep an eye on Frank and make sure he is safe. He's crazy. I think he likes nearly dying on every job we go to. I think it makes him feel alive or something.

The top of the staircase had a door to the roof, and boy, was it cold. I didn't mind. It made it easier to shoot. The plan was simple, Jazz Hands's room was right across from this building, and I could get a clean shot on him. Jazz had more people in his mob than ours, but they were all idiots. Street rats, mainly just looking to make a couple bucks and hold a gun while doing it. They were also sports geeks; it's all they ever talk about. Vic and Roger would strike up a conversation with the doormen about the Seattle baseball team, making sure that nobody else would get in the building. The thing that makes their gang so weak is that all the members relied so deeply on Jazz hands for orders. Every couple seconds, they would ask questions to him about what they had to do on a job, just annoying him in the process. Just like with any other job in the world, bosses don't want people who constantly ask questions about their job. They want people who will figure it out and do it effectively and quickly. If Jazz was out, then the whole building would crumble like a house of cards. I shoot Jazz through the window. The window breaking would be the signal for Vic and Roger to kill the doormen and then go inside to start picking off the people inside. I would shoot anybody trying to get out or people in windows, but the important thing was that nobody was allowed to leave. The building had three floors, all packed with girls, mobsters, and bartenders—none of them would live to tell the tale of tonight. Frank's orders.

Vic would get the $5 million that Jazz had in his room upstairs, and we would get out of here as fast as possible. All of this needed to happen in the next ten minutes, flawlessly.

Jazz was able to keep up his criminal escapades because he paid off the Seattle Police Department. The Seattle PD is corrupt so that you could get out of any crime, as long as you have the money. The biggest mafias in Seattle are able to get out of jail with ease. If you control the crime, then you control law enforcement too. With Jazz out of the way, the Miller family would walk away with $5 million in cash, police payoffs, and would be the top crime group in Seattle for years to come. If we pull this off, none of us would have to worry about anything ever again. All of us would have enough money to do anything we wanted. No more crime, no more killing, nothing.

I remember shooting with my dad as a kid. He always said I was pretty good. Whenever I feel down or stressed, I used to drive out of the city and shoot all day on my grandpa's ranch. Times change, though, and it seems that my shooting is now something more than a hobby.

"Are you ready, Vincent? Vic and Roger have been talking about ball games for the past three minutes to these guys. They don't suspect a thing." Fred was talking from the little walkie-talkie in my pocket

"Yeah, I'm ready." I had my rifle loaded and was getting ready to take the shot.

"All right, see you in ten."

Shooting is more calming than people think, mainly because the people that look down upon it seem to be on the other end of the rifle— at least that's the case in the mob. Jazz was in his room; I could see him through my scope—a large cigar in hand and hookers all around him. He was like a cat. A lazy beast benefiting from doing nothing. All of that was going to end. Chamber was loaded, the target was acquired, and after I had taken a deep breath, the plan was seemingly foolproof. And then Eric called.

BANG. Crack. The window broke, the hooker massaging Jazz's neck was dead. The boys on the doorstep got out the guns and took care of the doormen, and then they were in, having no idea that Jazz was alive. In panic, I picked up the portable phone that Eric forced me to get.

"Hey, honey, what's up?"

"Hey, I just put Olivia down for bed, I swear that kid just wants to stay up all night."

"Ha … yeah … I'll be home soon. I swear, these guys have me working overtime at the office tonight."

"Oh my god, I swear you are gonna work yourself to death."

"I know, I'll be home soon. Bye. 'Love you."

"'Love you."

I've been "married" to Eric for about three years now. No one really knows; they just assume we live together. We adopted Olivia a couple months ago, but times are tough in Seattle. Me and Eric lost our jobs, making both of us broke for a while. I told him I got this office job, but in actuality, I've been blowing guys' heads off their bodies. I love that man more than anything. I'd do anything for him, even join Seattle's crime family. I pack up my stuff and start running down to the van. I gotta get in there and help Victor and Roger quickly, or this whole operation is blown.

Fred was yelling on the walkie-talkie. "Vin, Roger says that the street rats are shooting at them inside. Did you whack Jazz or not?"

"I got a call. I missed the shot, but I'm on my way down there now. Are Vic and Roger having trouble?"

"Not right now, but you better get down here fast … Frank's gonna be pissed."

I've never run harder in my life. A chance at $5 million really changes a man. Vic took most of the weaponry in the van except for a shotgun, so I took that from Fred, and with my pistol in tow, I headed into the building.

Not even a couple feet in the door, a bloody man with a Seattle Seahawks jersey fires two shots at me. In his state, he couldn't hit anything. *Bang*, and he's out for good. The boys really went to town on the place. There wasn't a single seat in the house that wasn't occupied by a deceased partygoer. I felt as though I was going to hurl. Shots could be heard from above, but it was unclear if they were from our side. I decided to walk slowly across this first floor, which seems to be some sort of dance floor. Jazz Hands, as his name implies, likes a very select form of music, much more classy than your average mobster. Made him feel smart, I guess. The Seattle blues scene really benefited from it though, not tonight however. The stage where the Bacon Blues band played was deserted. The band looked as though it tried to get away, but the guitar player got a cap in his head before he could leave the stage. A shame. I have always loved the blues.

Vic was sometimes cruel in his methods, evidenced by the fact that the guy seemingly guarding the door was mangled beyond belief.

"How did he even do this?" I thought as I went up to the second floor.

Being in organized crime was tough. You had to deal with a lot of losses and violence. For some it's just too much. It seems downright over the top at some points. Victor had seen it all, is what people in the Miller family say. He was old—I don't know how old, but he had some years on him. His huge head of hair had a couple of grays in it, and he had seen most of what the American crime scene had to offer. Legends tell that he won some and he lost some, and lived to tell the tale of both. But I guess he would rather not talk about it, since no one really knows anything about him. Even so, how could somebody kill so violently.

I kill people, yeah, I do, but in a much more respectable manner. They blink, and they're gone. That's how I like to think about it, and just before I start feeling guilty, I get paid. Frank is a big fan of enlightened thinkers, reads books about those Renaissance guys all the time, and says "The ends justify the means" all the time. Easy for him to say. I've never seen him even punch a guy, let alone whack somebody. Before I opened the door to the second floor, I let some of the commotion die down. Sure, all this violence was partly my doing, but a lot of good it was gonna do me if the second I popped my head out, I was gone. Eventually the dust settled, and I was greeted by a huge barroom, filled with billiard tables and a seemingly endless supply of drinks. Some of these drinks were stolen from us a couple months ago by some of Jazz's goons. Frank was mad about that one. No one seemed to be around on this floor, so I had to go and meet the man himself.

"Vin!" I heard someone call from behind me

"Roger, there you are. Where's Victor?" I asked

Roger looked bad, almost as bad as some of the corpses around us. He came in with a blue blazer, but now it was covered in blood and cut beyond belief. He crumpled to the ground in a sort of a ball, and he looked as though he was crying.

"Roger, are you hurt? What happened?"

"Why is it that we do what we do?"

"What … what do you mean? Is Victor okay, where is—"

"I didn't want to kill him. I really didn't. He looked at me and said, 'Don't … please … I'll do anything,' but Victor said I had to, and he handed me this …" Roger picked up a sword that Victor must've brought in, covered in blood.

"He was crying and hugging his girl … but I just—" He started crying.

"Roger … I don't like it either, but we gotta get going. Now really isn't the time."

Nothing. He said nothing. I felt bad for him, I really did.

"You … just stay here. I'll go get Victor. Have a cigarette." I reach in my hand for my last one. Maybe it would calm him down.

"Sit here and breathe. I'll be back."

He took it and lit it, but the smoke didn't come without a couple of tears as well. I just couldn't shake that question. *Why do I do this?*

The second flight of stairs, the last of them. The gunshots had ceased from upstairs; someone had won and someone had lost. I peered through the crack of the door leading to Jazz's room. Nothing. Not a sight or sound. Opening the door, I saw no blood or corpses on the floor—a breath of fresh air compared to what was downstairs. Victor opened the door, and I found myself staring down the barrel of one of his huge revolvers.

"Oh … hi, Vin," he said as he put the big gun away. "Are you hurt? Where is Roger?"

"I'm fine. Roger is downstairs having a smoke. You have the money?"

"Right here." He lifted a duffel bag that looked as though it was about to burst open due to the amount of cash in it. "Everyone in the building is dead. We better hurry before the cops get here."

Victor had a cigar in his mouth that he was puffing, presumably Jazz Hands's last cigar. In the Miller family, smoking is a sign of masculinity and experience. Only the truly powerful smoke cigars, but the deadly smoke cigars that were once in the mouths of villains.

"Vic, do you think Frank is gonna be mad at me for missing the shot."

"I don't think so, we finished the job at the end of the day, and all of us are alive."

"Okay … Vic, why do you do this?"

No response. Victor looked at me, I think (I couldn't see his face through his hair), and simply puffed his cigar. Pondering the question, he sat down on the floor for a minute. He unzipped the duffel bag, making sure everything was in order.

"I do this line of work because it makes me happy. I know it sounds crazy, but this work makes me feel alive for once. I've had a long life, but nothing makes me happier than taking care of bad people."

"Bad people? You mean Jazz or the street rats?"

"Both. We are the good guys, and good guys win. That's what Frank tells us, right?"

"Yeah, I guess that makes sense."

"Now let's hurry. We have to finish our game of blackjack."

He stood up and started toward the door, but not before turning around and throwing the cigar back to its rightful owner.

PEACE MACHINE

Everybody knew that the world was split in two, Blue and Green. The insignificant lives of the many outweigh the long, fruitful lives of the few. John knew this better than anyone. Now, staring into Death's eyes at the end of his short life, he has only one purpose: to feed the Machine.

Nobody knew when the Machine gained total control, but everyone knew of its inception. Legends say that around the twenty-first century, during the Third World War, all the nations came together to make an AI to stop the carnage going on around them. Its solution: Everyone picks a side. The Machine promised peace for all as long as it was obeyed, and for centuries, this godless and meaningless planet known as Earth had one savior, the Machine.

John knew that Blue was the righteous side and Green was the wrong side. This was taught to him at a young age, and he knew that all of his hatred of the Greens would be bottled up inside him and released into the Machine in just a couple hours. He woke up, ate breakfast, showered, and was on his way to the Blue Headquarters to fulfill his destiny. The Blue District of the last remaining city on Earth was bustling, as it usually was, with people going in all directions imaginable, kids wandering, and a riot or two. It was all normal and mundane to him. The people of the last remaining city felt only three emotions: hate, greed, and anger—all directed toward the Green portion of the city. No one ever ventured there, for fear of being mauled to death by people vouching for their righteous side.

Throughout human history, everyone's thoughts on life and this world could be boiled down to two categories, though those categories are always changing. Good versus evil, Coke versus Pepsi, religion, politics, mostly meaningless things. People would fight over all for some pointless conjecture and dominance. The Machine knew that this is what separates man and animal, and thus split the world in two using the thing that every human could relate to and fight for—music. When the Machine was fed by those who believe in the righteous side of the Green or the Blue, music was made. Music that kept people going, kept them happy. When the people of the last city heard the Music of the Machine, they were reminded of why they lived, and thus they wanted the Machine to keep making it.

Despite this, everyone must pick a side, from the ages of four to fifteen. Everyone represented their preferred music. John would be Blue until he drew his last breath, he was sure of it. As he passed all the same familiar places that he did as kid, he was reminded why he was fighting the good fight. It was just a fact to John at this point. *Their way of life is wrong, and ours is the path the Machine wants us to follow.* He kept thinking as he made his way to the headquarters of the Blue that his life was meaningless if not for the Machine. He had no friends, no family, nothing but the clothes on his back, and the apartment he lived in to call his own. He hated everyone and everything, including himself. The only person he had some compassion for was the little girl on the third block of the last city.

Penny was a special kid. She had wide eyes, pigtails, and brown hair. She was thrown out of the Green subdivision a couple of years ago. The Blue officers thought of her as just one more person to feed the Machine and end this godforsaken war, so she was adopted into the Blue subdivision at the age of four. Everyone saw her as the village weirdo. She had never expressed any of the normal emotions felt by people of the righteous path. While some civilians are able to go on long elaborate essays about their way of life, Penny had never spoken of either side.

Many thought she would never be able to fit in, seeing as she was from the Green side. People at first tried to teach her of their ways, how to worship the Machine and become a good feeder, but Penny never seemed to grasp that concept. All she did every day was try to plant flowers on a little patch of soil near her apartment. In a world where people worshiped a Machine, nature was hard to come by in the last city, many people going their whole lives never even seeing a branch of a tree.

Penny would go out every day and watch them grow, whispering to herself, "We all are going to go someday."

Everyone hated her. People kept her around as either a source of comedy or just another reason to hate the Green side. People would throw rocks at her, stomp her flowers, and thrash her pretty much every day. With all her bruises, she was nearly unrecognizable some days. Blood dripping from her face, tears in her eyes, and dead flowers were all products of going against the Machine.

John saw Penny every day on his walk. Rain, snow, drought—it didn't matter. She was always there. He turned at all the same spots and passed all the same people and places on his way to her house, and when he finally made it, she wasn't there. No one was there, only a white tulip sprouting from the ground. Looking down at the flower, John realized how small it truly was—an insignificant little speck of life compared to him.

Why on earth does Penny give a damn about a stupid little flower, John said to himself as he crushed it. He thought maybe it was a kid thing and tried to recall childhood memories of his.

He was fifteen now. His parents were fed at a young age, and he had to live on his own. He never remembered doing any of what Penny did when he was young. Don't get him wrong, John hated Penny as much as the next guy, but there was something so innocent and naive about her, that made him disappointed not to see her today. But it didn't matter. Today he would say goodbye to all of that as he fed the Machine. Penny was too young to understand anything of significance. Unlike Penny, John had a grasp on his life.

At that moment, exactly noon on a Sunday, right when John arrived at the headquarters, the music started playing. It played only once a month, and everyone savored the moment. John saw pedestrians stop in their tracks, drop their suitcases and possessions, get on the ground, and listen.

As the clock struck on the headquarters' clock, the heavenly symphony that the savior of Earth had to offer started playing. John sat down on the steps of the building and listened. He imagined a warmth that he never had from his parents, friends he never made, happiness he never achieved. He started crying,

John had waited for this moment all his life. Now it had finally arrived, it was finally here. All the cruelty of this world, the violence he saw on the streets, the hatred—it would all be a distant memory soon. For the first time in his life, John was happy. He cried and rocked himself back and forth, knowing it would all be over soon. He wouldn't have to be a burden anymore, and he wasn't going to continue being just another mouth to feed for the people of the Blue District. As the song played, he finally had a purpose.

Others cried and wept around him, hugging themselves and smiling. And then, just as quickly as it began, the song ended, and everyone wiped their faces and went about their day. John wiped the tears from his face, got up, and faced the future that was in store for him. He approached the doors of the building. It had a poster on it that said, "Our numbers are down, consider feeding today." The poster had a smiling woman on it, with blonde hair and blue eyes, and nearly every piece of her outfit had the emblem of the Machine and a tint of blue in it. John opened the door and was soon stuck in a long line of people, who were all here for the same reason.

John waited and waited, and waited, and reflected on his life—what little of it he truly had. He had woken up and done the same mundane and meaningless things that everyone had done in this city. Nobody in this city ever did anything of significance, nor did they ever have any fun or happiness in their life. John couldn't remember the last time he smiled, except, of course when the music was playing. It always seemed that he was pulled out of his life when it started playing. Like a bird flying away, he too left his body for just a couple of moments every time it played. He imagined death would be much the same: No more of this world, no more hate, no more Penny. Just him and the Machine. It sounded like paradise, but then the music stopped, and he was back.

"Can I help you?" a lady asked John, taking him out of his own little world.

"Yeah, I'm on the list to be fed today."

She started looking around her desk for a piece of paper. The lady looked as though she was trying to pull off the same look as the lady on the poster, but it just was not working. She had blue all over her as expected, but her hair really didn't match her clothes at all. Not that it mattered. This lady was one of the last people anybody saw before death. What she wore was hardly anyone's concern.

"John Morgan, scheduled for noon—is this you?"

"Uh, yeah, that's me"

"Go through the door and shut it on your way out. Say hi to the Machine and follow his instructions. Thank you and have a nice day," the lady said halfheartedly as she turned back to her computer. With this final registration, John had nothing more to do, see, feel, or become. He had burned all his bridges and was ready for his destiny. So why, he kept asking, did he do what he did next?

"Hey, um could you do me a favor? There's this little girl on the third block ... could you tell her that ... well, tell her that she should really consider the cause we're fighting for."

The woman thought to herself first and then said, "Oh, you mean Penny? She killed herself this morning."

"What?"

"Yeah, that weird girl with the pigtails. She jumped off a building this morning. The police were getting ready to kick her out of the Blue District this morning, and they found her on the other side of town like that."

"Oh, well … never mind, then."

"What a shame, huh? One more body to feed the Machine never goes to waste, but if you ask me"—the woman leaned in closer and whispered—"that kid was the village weirdo, a little Green block in an otherwise perfect blue city."

"Haha, uh, yeah. Well, thanks anyway."

"Whatever." The woman went back to work as if nothing happened, as if she didn't just crush John's only hope for this world.

John had nothing left to do. He thought as he walked to the Machine, *Why did he ask that lady to talk to Penny?* He knew more than anyone that Penny was hopeless. Nothing would ever change her. As fast and frequently as this world changed, Penny would always remain a constant. So why did he ask such a stupid question? More importantly, why did he care? He and Penny had never even said anything to each other. Hell, Penny probably didn't know he existed. That little twerp on the third block did nothing for anybody. She never loved or hated anything or anyone, and John didn't like knowing that a person like that was gone. Even though it didn't matter, even though the Machine was his future, even though the Blue music would ring a month from now as though nothing happened at all, John missed Penny.

Well, we all gotta go someday, he kept thinking as he closed the door to the Machine's room.

John was now standing in a dark hallway, pipes on the walls leading to the only source of light he could see—a turquoise block of light at the end of the hallway through a little doorway. He felt the rusty old pipes along the walls as he walked; the dials, buttons, lights, and screws were all foreign to him, technology from the past. He could hear a faint rendition of the Blue music coming from the end of the hallway, compelling him. It was much softer than the rendition he heard this morning, much brighter and slightly faster as well. He tried to think of all the things he would say to the Machine, all the ways he would thank him for giving peace to the world, that despite the low numbers of people, Blue would triumph.

Trying to hold back tears of joy from the beautiful tune he heard, he made his way down to the hallway, stepped through the door, and saw the Machine for the first time. Unlike the machinery leading him there, the Machine seemed to be this chrome, nearly mirrorlike giant figure. It was lit up with this beautiful sea greenish/bluish color that moved as if they were waves in the ocean, with what seemed like brush strokes of black at the tips of each color, making it seem as though the Machine had this depth to it.

"A sea of cool colors and symphony of souls," was how the Machine was described. He had no eyes, for he saw all, nor did he have any other humanlike features, except for a tiny little doggy door at the bottom. It was rusty and bent. You could see sharp spikes, girders, and rods move inside the doggy door. Other than this little detail, the Machine was heavenly— no, it was heaven itself. The more John looked at it the more he wanted to help it and the more he wanted to serve his purpose.

Hello, John, how are you?

The Machine said this in a calm and friendly voice, like an old high school buddy that you would run into after not seeing them for years. John was shaking in his blue shoes. He didn't know how to respond, all while this heavenly music played in the background. It all just seemed so perfect. He had never been happier.

You seem to be anxious. Do not be afraid, this process will be over soon.

"I ... thank you . . . thank you so much for everything you have given me. I love you."

You are welcome. Come now, we haven't much time to lose.

John stepped closer to the Machine, a smile on his face. He was ready for whatever was to come next.

Good, now get in a crawling position and crawl through the small window in front of you.

Doing as he was told, he got a good look at what was through the doggy door. He saw blood everywhere, not a single spot not covered in a red paintlike substance. He could see another doggy door on the other side, and he assumed it was for the Green District's side, seeing as their headquarters shared the same building. He was scared; he thought this would be a little quicker and painless.

"Is this going to hurt, Machine?"

No, it will not hurt, it will be over before you know it, now get in a crawling position and crawl through the small window in front of you.

"Okay … and, uh, thanks again for everything you have done. I mean, if it wasn't for you, I would have shot myself or something. You have given me a greater purpose. Thanks."

You are welcome. Now get in a crawling position and crawl through the small window in front of you.

John took a deep breath and did as he was told. He got to die listening to his favorite song, with a smile on his face, and finally feeling as though he was happy.

However, this was a lie. The truth is that John's life was stolen from him—stolen by an insecure and scared society worshiping a byproduct of a bloodier war than the little body-chopping doggy door room that John was now in. He had served his purpose in this life. In another, he was a husband and a father to the family he loved. In another, he was a chef, a doctor, a veterinarian, a teacher—you name it. John could have been somebody, but he wasn't. The Machine was still standing, though, and it would continue to feed off the depressed, hopeless Johns of this pointless and meaningless world, for years and years as Pennys come and go.

The Machine would feed on both sides of the city for centuries and centuries until all the flowers were stomped, all the secretaries have gone, and there was no more pain in the world. The Machine would feed until there was nothing but him and Blue and Green music.

Inspired by Georgia O'Keeffe's *Blue and Green Music*

Love yourself, or you'll go crazy trying to figure out everything else

Thank you